W9-BJK-574

For Rachel Claire
M.W.

For Genevieve and Asher
B.F.

First U.S. edition in this format 2008

Library of Congress Cataloging-in-Publication Data is available.

Library of Congress Catalog Card Number 91-071858

ISBN 978-0-7636-4036-1

2 4 6 8 10 9 7 5 3 1

Printed in China

This book was typeset in Monotype Columbus.
The illustrations were done in watercolor, ink and pencil.

Candlewick Press
2067 Massachusetts Avenue
Cambridge, Massachusetts 02140

CANDLEWICK PRESS
2067 MASSACHUSETTS AVENUE
CAMBRIDGE MA 02140

Can't You Sleep, Little Bear?

Martin Waddell

illustrated by Barbara Firth

Once there were two bears,
Big Bear and Little Bear.
Big Bear is the big bear, and Little Bear is the little bear. They played all day in the bright sunlight. When night came, and the sun went down, Big Bear took Little Bear home to the Bear Cave.

Big Bear put Little Bear to bed in the dark part of the cave. “Go to sleep, Little Bear,” he said.

And Little Bear tried.

Big Bear settled in the Bear Chair and read his Bear Book by the light of the fire.

But Little Bear couldn’t get to sleep.

"Can't you sleep, Little Bear?"
asked Big Bear, putting down his Bear Book
(which was just getting to the interesting part) and
padding over to the bed.

"I'm scared," said Little Bear.

"Why are you scared, Little Bear?" asked Big Bear.

"I don't like the dark," said Little Bear.

"What dark?" said Big Bear.

"The dark all around us,"
said Little Bear.

Big Bear looked, and he saw that the dark part of the cave was very dark, so he went to the Lantern Cupboard and took out the tiniest lantern that was there.

Big Bear lit the tiniest lantern, and put it next to Little Bear's bed.

"There's a tiny light to keep you from being scared, Little Bear," said Big Bear.

"Thank you, Big Bear," said Little Bear, cuddling up in the glow.

"Now go to sleep, Little Bear," said Big Bear, and he padded back to the Bear Chair and settled down to read the Bear Book by the light of the fire.

Little Bear tried to go to sleep, but he couldn't.

"Can't you sleep, Little Bear?" yawned Big Bear, putting down his Bear Book (with just four pages to go to the interesting part) and padding over to the bed.

"I'm scared," said Little Bear.

"Why are you scared, Little Bear?" asked Big Bear.

"I don't like the dark," said Little Bear.

"What dark?" asked Big Bear.

"The dark all around us," said Little Bear.

"But I brought you a lantern!" said Big Bear.

"Only a teeny-weeny one," said Little Bear. "And there's lots of dark!"

Big Bear looked, and he saw that Little Bear was quite right. There was still lots of dark. So Big Bear went to the Lantern Cupboard and took out a bigger lantern.

Big Bear lit the lantern and put it beside the other one.

“Now go to sleep, Little Bear,”
said Big Bear, and he padded back to the Bear Chair
and settled down to read the Bear Book
by the light of the fire.

Little Bear tried and tried to go to sleep,
but he couldn't.

"Can't you sleep,
Little Bear?"
grunted Big Bear, putting
down his Bear Book
(with just three pages to go)
and padding over to the bed.

"I'm scared," said Little Bear.

"Why are you scared, Little Bear?" asked Big Bear.

"I don't like the dark," said Little Bear.

"What dark?" asked Big Bear.

"The dark all around us," said Little Bear.

"But I brought you two lanterns!" said Big Bear. "A tiny one and a bigger one!"

"Not much bigger," said Little Bear. "And there's still lots of dark."

Big Bear thought about it, and then he went to the Lantern Cupboard and took out the Biggest Lantern of Them All, with two handles and a piece of chain. He hooked up the lantern above Little Bear's bed.

"I've brought you the Biggest Lantern of Them All!" he told Little Bear. "That's to keep you from being scared!"

"Thank you, Big Bear," said Little Bear, curling up in the glow and watching the shadows dance.

"Now go to sleep, Little Bear," said Big Bear, and he padded back to the Bear Chair and settled down to read the Bear Book by the light of the fire.

Little Bear tried and tried and
tried to go to sleep,
but he couldn't.

"Can't you sleep, Little Bear?" groaned Big Bear,
putting down his Bear Book
(with just two pages to go)
and padding over to the bed.

“I’m scared,” said Little Bear.

“Why are you scared, Little Bear?” asked Big Bear.

“I don’t like the dark,” said Little Bear.

“What dark?” asked Big Bear.

“The dark all around us,” said Little Bear.

“But I brought you the Biggest Lantern of Them All, and there isn’t any dark left,” said Big Bear.

“Yes, there is!” said Little Bear. “There is. Out there!” And he pointed out of the Bear Cave at the night.

Big Bear saw that Little Bear was right. Big Bear was very puzzled. All the lanterns in the world couldn't light up the dark outside.

Big Bear thought about it for a long time, and then he said, "Come on, Little Bear."

"Where are we going?" asked Little Bear.

"Out!" said Big Bear.

"Out into the darkness?" said Little Bear.

"Yes!" said Big Bear.

"But I'm scared of the dark!" said Little Bear.

"No need to be!" said Big Bear, and he took Little Bear by the paw and led him out of the cave into the night

and it was . . .

DARK!

“Ooooh! I’m scared,” said Little Bear,
cuddling up to Big Bear.
Big Bear lifted Little Bear and
cuddled him and said, “Look at the dark,
Little Bear.” And Little Bear looked.

"I've brought you the moon, Little Bear," said Big Bear. "The bright yellow moon and all the twinkly stars."

But Little Bear didn't say anything, for he had gone to sleep, warm and safe in Big Bear's arms.

Big Bear carried Little Bear back into the Bear Cave, fast asleep, and he settled down with Little Bear on one arm and the Bear Book on the other, cozy in the Bear Chair by the fire.

And Big Bear read the Bear Book right to . . .

THE END